P9-DMG-256

FIN TITLES YOU MAY ENJOY

Growing up isn't

Thinking is one ...
between these Co...
of mine, ain't no...

CeCe hates i...
She swears I'...
and imagine...
otherwise.

A pair...
1960's, ...
told Ce...
tryin...
"Th...

OTHER PUF

Fast Sam, Cool C...
Gr...
Let the Circle ...
Roll of Thunder...
Won't Know Till I ...

Jazmin's notebook

Nikki Grimes

PUFFIN BOOKS

NEW HANOVER COUNTY
PUBLIC LIBRARY
201 CHESTNUT STREET
WILMINGTON. NC 28401

PUFFIN BOOKS
Published by the Penguin Group
Penguin Putnam Books for Young Readers,
345 Hudson Street, New York, New York 10014, U.S.A.
Penguin Books Ltd, 27 Wrights Lane, London W8 5TZ, England
Penguin Books Australia Ltd, Ringwood, Victoria, Australia
Penguin Books Canada Ltd, 10 Alcorn Avenue, Toronto, Ontario, Canada M4V 3B2
Penguin Books (N.Z.) Ltd, 182-190 Wairau Road, Auckland 10, New Zealand

Penguin Books Ltd, Registered Offices: Harmondsworth, Middlesex, England

First published in the United States of America by Dial Books,
a member of Penguin Putnam Inc., 1998
Published by Puffin Books,
a member of Penguin Putnam Books for Young Readers, 2000

19 20

Copyright © Nikki Grimes, 1998
All rights reserved

THE LIBRARY OF CONGRESS HAS CATALOGED THE DIAL EDITION AS FOLLOWS:
Grimes, Nikki.
Jazmin's notebook / Nikki Grimes.
p. cm.
Summary: Jazmin, an African-American teenager who lives with her sister in
a small Harlem apartment in the 1960's, finds strength in writing poetry
and keeping a record of the events in her sometimes difficult life.
ISBN 0-8037-2224-9
1. Afro-Americans—Juvenile fiction. [1. Afro-Americans—Fiction.
2. Authorship—Fiction. 3. Poetry—Fiction. 4. Diaries—Fiction. 5. Sisters—Fiction.
6. Harlem (New York, N.Y.)—Fiction.] I. Title.
PZ7.G88429Jan 1998 [Fic]—dc21 97-5850 CIP AC

Puffin Books ISBN 0-14-130702-1

Printed in the United States of America

Except in the United States of America, this book is sold subject to the condition that
it shall not, by way of trade or otherwise, be lent, re-sold, hired out, or otherwise
circulated without the publisher's prior consent in any form of binding or cover
other than that in which it is published and without a similar condition
including this condition being imposed on the subsequent purchaser.

For my sister, Carol,
who helped me beat the odds.

Acknowledgments

I am deeply grateful to my editor, Toby Sherry, for her wise guidance, enthusiastic support, and unflagging faith in this project.

Many thanks, as well, go to her former assistant, Victoria Wells, for her sharp-eyed observations and helpful notes.

I also owe a debt of gratitude to poet Rasul Murray, authors Ann Braybrook and Michelle Y. Green, and friend Toppin Martin. Their perceptive questions, comments, and suggestions helped me tremendously. Thanks, guys!

First, last, and always, I thank God for allowing me to do the work that I love.

Jazmin's notebook

*A*ccording to my sister, CeCe, the night before I was born, Mom and Dad sat in the living room, timing Mom's early contractions and arguing about my name during the minutes in between. They both agreed on the name itself, but spent half the night fighting about the spelling.

CeCe was six years old at the time, and would have been fast asleep, except that the tenement our family lived in on Lenox & 133rd was the size of a Cracker Jack box, with walls twice as thin, and sound carried easily from room to room. CeCe, in bed at the other end of the apartment, remembers laying wide-awake that night, lis-

3

tening to every word. She couldn't understand everything she heard, of course, but years later Mom filled in the details.

Apparently my father wanted my name to be a sort of homage to jazz. He sold insurance for a living, but he was a frustrated sax man, and he figured if he couldn't spend his life playing jazz, he at least ought to be able to honor his love of "America's only original art form" by making it part of his baby daughter's name. He said this while Duke Ellington's "Sophisticated Lady" serenaded Mom from the stereo, mind you, so it's no wonder she got the hint. "Fine," she said. "We're well into the 50's, so why not *really* be modern and use a *y* in place of the *i*, while you're at it." But Dad said that was carrying uniqueness a bit too far. "Besides," he argued, "with a *y* instead of an *i*, people would be confused about the right way to pronounce the name." He won the argument, eventually, and so my birth certificate reads Jazmin Shelby. That's Jazmin with a *z*.

Now, that phrase might sound cute, but sometimes I find it downright annoying because I know I'll have to go through life repeating it over and over again. No one seems to get the spelling right on the first or second try.

I think it's great that Mom and Dad went to the trouble of making my name unique. But I've often considered changing it to Sally, or Linda, or maybe Jane, as in "See

Jane run." That's one spelling everyone can manage. Of course, that kind of name wouldn't last me any longer than my straight perm did because I'm my own me, nappy hair and all, and truth is, Jazmin suits me best.

Folks will figure out how to spell my name sooner or later, I suppose, especially after they see it splashed across the jacket of my future best-seller (smile). Meanwhile, I've got my work cut out.

THE GARDEN OF EDEN

Day and night
the electric sizzle
of the neon sign
hisses its invitation:
"Come on in.
If you have the price,
we'll sell you a pint
of paradise."

APRIL 16

You can be right next door to paradise and not even know it. I think about that sometimes when I sit here warming up the stoop, surveying Amsterdam Avenue from my self-styled post, smack between the Laundromat and The Garden of Eden Bar & Grill.

The bar & grill blasts rhythm and blues on the juke-box all hours of the night, while cocaine changes hands in dark corners, and pool-sharks in the back room beat amateurs out of a week's pay. The Garden of Eden has its

6

share of snakes, so you might say it's an angel or two shy of heaven. But the name sure gets you thinking, and thinking is one thing I'm good at. Just as well since, between these Coke-bottle spectacles and these chicken-legs of mine, ain't nobody inviting me out to dance.

CeCe hates it when I denigrate myself out loud that way. She swears I'm beautiful, mainly because she's my big sister and imagines that's her job. I don't have the heart to tell her otherwise.

A pair of contact lenses would help my cause. It's the 1960's, for God's sake. Nearly everybody's wearing them. I told CeCe this. Okay, so it's a slight exaggeration, but I was trying to make a point. CeCe yawned and shook her head. "That's my baby," she said. "Always good for a laugh."

Every once in a while I slip downstairs in a scoop-neck sweater and tight hip-hugger jeans, minus my specs, in hopes of drawing a bit of positive male atten-tion. It works too. Of course, I'm blind as a bat, so Lord help me if I'm doing laundry that day. I have to dig around in my pocket, pry out coins for the washer and dryer, and choose the right ones by *feel*—either that or pull out a handful of coins, and squint, which kind of de-feats the purpose.

I swear, I'm not planning on being this vain and shal-low all my life. Just 'til I get through high school.

AMSTERDAM AVENUE

Siren screams and car horns
clog the air.
Still, the sparrow's song
survives the blare.
And, though six-storied buildings
crowd this sky,
The sun scissors through and shines—
and so will I.

A spring rain threatened late this afternoon, and except for J.D., the numbers runner down at the newsstand, and four girls jumping double-dutch in front of the Laundromat, the street was pretty empty. I hope J.D. wasn't trying to be inconspicuous, because the red, black, and green dashiki he was wearing didn't do the trick. It was a gray day, and J.D.'s shirt stood out like bright paint splashes on a charcoal page. I found myself staring at him until I realized it wasn't J.D. that caught my eye, but his shirt. Not that I needed a wild dashiki print to hold my attention. I wasn't exactly itching to go inside, and there was no reason to rush since, by some miracle, I'd escaped from school without any homework. *Hallelujah!*

CeCe says I spend way too much time on this stoop, but I can't help it. Living in rooming houses off and on, and sleeping three in a bed for most of the years that we were small, has made me a freak for space. I've got no say in the size of the place we live in. I'm lucky to have a place at all, with Mom back in the hospital. But that doesn't change the fact that I feel cramped inside our tiny one-and-a-half bedroom apartment. At least down on the stoop I can stretch my arms out in either direction without making contact with a wall, or a chest of drawers, or another living soul. I take what I can get.

Amsterdam Avenue has a wideness that'll fool you. You get the idea that there's plenty of space—space for every kind of person, every kind of dream. Wrong. I've lived on or near Amsterdam Avenue in Sugar Hill and up here in Washington Heights, and I'm not buying it. I see Woolworth's scraping shoulders with Safeway, and Sherman's Bar-B-Q elbowing the record store for room. The beauty salons and barbershops, drugstores and candy shops, funeral parlors and storefront churches all seem to be jamming each other in the ribs to create an inch or two of breathing space. You need a magnifying glass to find a library, though, or a bookstore, and those are the places where my visions come alive. But the Avenue doesn't seem to have much room for them.

Looks like my dreams and I will have to fight for space. But that's okay. I was born with clenched fists.

42ND STREET LIBRARY

The library
is no place to kneel
but this cathedral of books
feels holy.
I observe
a moment of silence
at the entryway.
The librarians
like ushers
point me in
the right direction.
I've only been here
once before.
That first time
I was a human top
spinning dizzy
in the middle of the hall.
I thought all visitors
should bow
or fold their hands—
do something special.

But I was too
dazed myself
to do more than
gaze up, and up, and up
and sigh.
The "Quiet" signs
posted everywhere
warned me not to speak.
And why would I want to?
It looked to me like
all the good words
were already taken.

MAY 9
___

It must've been 6:15 when Aunt Sarah came home tonight. I'm convinced the sun sets itself by her timely comings and goings. She trudged up the Avenue from a long day of emptying bedpans and dispensing prescriptions at Columbia Presbyterian.

Her body sagged as if the stiffness of her starched white nurse's uniform was all that held her up. "Hi, baby," she said, her voice warm as a cuddle. "How you doin' today?"

"Pretty good."

"And how's the writing coming along?"

I paused long enough to smile and answer. "Fine, Aunt Sarah."

"That's good. That's good. You keep it up, hear?"

"I will," I said.

"You oughta send some of that fine writing to your mama in the hospital. I bet she'd enjoy that." Aunt Sarah means well, but Mom is in no shape to be reading poetry from me or anybody else at the moment. She's so deep inside herself, CeCe says the doctors are thinking about giving her shock treatment. I didn't tell any of this to Aunt Sarah, though. I just smiled.

By then she was at the top of the stairs. I held the door open for her, watched her disappear inside.

Too bad Aunt Sarah's not my real aunt. She's so nice, I wouldn't mind having her as a relative. Maybe that's why everyone around here calls her "Aunt." She's got her own family, of course. A daughter, and two grandkids. I'd be glad to substitute for them anytime. Lord knows Aunt Sarah's had a hug with my name on it every day since CeCe and I moved into the apartment next to hers. And her caring also shows up on our table, steaming from a bowl heaped with collard greens and kale. Leftovers she calls them, but we all know better. They only appear when CeCe is low on cash.

I've called 2104 Amsterdam Avenue home going on a

year now. I've been sent postage-paid to so many different relatives and foster homes over the last fourteen years that I've lived in every borough of New York City at least twice, so one year in the same place is close to being a record.

It's hard to keep track of all the places I've known, all the faces, which is the real reason I'm keeping this notebook. I'm tired of losing people before I even have a chance to commit their names to memory.

Aunt Sarah is a name that spells kindness, and when I leave this place, hers is one name I plan on taking with me.

MAY 20

*E*very time a guy waltzes up the Avenue sporting a beret, I see Daddy, especially if the beret is black and worn the way his was, with a jazzy tilt to the side. Like that man who leapt, pantherlike, from the 101 bus today, and headed in my direction.

My heart somersaulted two, three times at least, then pushed the word "Daddy" to the tip of my tongue. But only for one split-second. Then logic gave the word a shove, and left me choking.

Stupid! I said to myself. *What's wrong with you? Daddy died in that car crash going on a year. You oughta be clear on that by now.*

The closer the stranger got to the stoop, the sillier I felt, because, apart from the beret, he was dressed all wrong. His jacket matched his pants, which Daddy's never did, he wore a tailored black wool coat, not a trench, and to top it off, he was a full six inches too short! But that beret had me going. I watched it until the hat and the man disappeared around the corner.

Come to think of it, the bus should have clued me in that I was dreaming. Daddy drove his own car, and was plenty proud of it. Mind you, he had no use for the pink Lincolns or the mile-long, fire-engine-red Cadillacs other men parade down the Avenue, but he sure wasn't above cruising in his black MG to show it off. Shoot! He wouldn't have been caught riding a city bus if his life depended on it.

CeCe says my sense of irony has developed quite a bit here lately. I suppose she's got a point.

FOR SALE

I pass the used-goods store
peek at
the bronzed baby shoes
useless and dusty
in the window.
It's legal
to sell such things,
I know.
But it feels wrong
to me,
someone selling
someone else's
memory.

It must drive God crazy to see how much we take for granted. My friend Jabari is a great example. This afternoon his grandmother left Wilson's Drugstore, grinning, and hurried across the Avenue clutching a large envelope.

She stopped in front of The Garden to catch her breath, and waved me over while she rested. "Looka here," she said, slipping an 8 x 10 glossy from the envelope. It was a photo from Jabari's prom.

"That's my grandbaby!" she said, proud as the First Lady, going on about how clever she knew he was, and how he got his brains from *her* side of the family, and how she planned on framing his diploma—in silver, no less. Man! You'd think he had graduated from Harvard, instead of being on his way to high school along with the rest of us. Then again he might be the first in his family to make it so far. Whether he is or not, I suppose his grandmother has the right to brag.

I smiled politely and said, yes, Jabari did look mighty handsome in that fine suit. Which is right about when she dug out her wallet and rewarded my good manners by showing me an old photograph of Jabari, scooting, bare-bottomed, across a baby blanket.

"He always was the cutest thing," she cooed.

All I could think was, *Poor Jabari!* What's this thing grown-ups have about showing off embarrassing pictures of naked babies? I don't know. I couldn't keep from laughing, though. After all, this is the guy I sometimes meet on the basketball court after school, for a game of one-on-one. Now, thanks to seeing that photo, I'll never be able to look at his sweaty, muscled, six-foot frame quite the same again. And it didn't help that Jabari showed up while tears of laughter were still streaming down my cheeks.

Can't much blame him for snatching that wallet right out of his grandma's hands. I'd have done the same.

But, trust me: Jabari ought to be counting his blessings. There are no photos of *me* as a baby, carefully pasted in a family album. No sweet portrait on a mantel beside a pair of bronzed baby shoes. There are no Kodak memories of *my* third birthday party, face happily smeared with cake frosting, or strawberry ice cream. There are no wallet-size proofs of my existence at the age of eight. Or nine. Or ten. I wish there were.

Some foster homes are pretty okay, but you can't have pictures if you barely live with folks long enough to learn their address. They've got no reason to take them. Of course, it's different now that I'm with CeCe. She takes lots of pictures, pictures of me, of me with my friends Destinee and Sophie, pictures of CeCe and me together. In fact, she's gone a little picture crazy, if you ask me. Still, it's hard to keep track of a little thing like a photograph when you're constantly moving. Stuff gets left behind. No one can help that. Not even CeCe.

So I'm not taking any chances. These words, these notes are gonna be my photographs of me. Of who I am, and what I do, and what my life is like. Here. Now.

Someday I'll look at this photograph of me, and Jabari, and his oh-so-proud grandmother, and I'll grin. The way I'm grinning now.

● · ● ·

 've got mixed feelings about UFOs and aliens, but I've had a number of close encounters in my life, and I know I'm not the first. There's this lady I call Sister Church, because I see her on the way from one each Sunday and I've noticed the secret sparkle she has in her eye, as if she's seen or heard something that no one else has.

She high-stepped down the Avenue earlier today, uniformed in white to match the other women of New Jerusalem Sanctuary of the Redeemed, over on St. Nicholas. White straw hat, white cotton gloves clutched in her hand, blazing white short-sleeve dress, white bag, and white shoes. You know, those flat, orthopedic-looking numbers. Nurse's shoes maybe. Either way, they gleamed like snow.

I'm not exactly sure what white has to do with God. I understand the connection with purity, of course. Ivory soap, 99 and 44/100 % pure, etcetera. Fine. I get it. Still, when I look at the world God made, I get the distinct impression that He's partial to color. Sister Church does look good in white, though. Cool, too, on this warm May day.

Shawna was on the stoop with me when Sister Church danced by, high on the spirit, bubbling over with what CeCe calls "the zeal of the Lord."

"Good afternoon," she greeted, mopping her brow with a lace kerchief. White, of course. "How y'all young folks doin' today?"

"Fine," I said, answering for both of us. Shawna was too busy snickering to be polite.

"I believe the Good Lord gave me a message for you this mornin'. He spoke to me. Yes, He did. He said, 'I have given angels charge over thee.'" Her words sent a tingle up my spine, but Shawna just rolled her eyes. "Lady, you must be hearin' voices again, 'cause ain't no God tell you nothin'. If there *is* a God," she added, rubbing her swollen belly. The small life inside gave her a walloping kick.

Good, I thought. *Serves you right.* Then I remembered what CeCe says: Be patient with people. We all believe what we know, or what we can, or what we want to.

Believing in close encounters of the spiritual kind comes easily to me, partly because CeCe was born with second sight, and I've been hearing about visions and prophetic dreams all my life, and partly because I've met and talked to angels on more than one occasion, and found their presence so matter-of-fact that I assumed other people saw them too. I've learned not to talk about such things. I don't enjoy being laughed at.

Still, there's a lot that happens in this life that people can't explain. Like why CeCe could be in Jersey, and I could be in Ossining, New York, and every time she gets a stomachache, I do too. Or what happened the time CeCe and I were in that foster home on Long Island and ran away because the woman beat us.

I was three years old then, but I remember how we skipped down the street so no one would notice we were leaving. And how, once we turned the corner, our feet flew. The next thing I knew, we were inside of Mom's apartment in Manhattan, standing at the window, waving to her as she came home. Shocked to find us there, she raced upstairs, shoved her key in the door, and discovered that it was still locked. From the outside.

The trip itself was part of the mystery. There were no bus rides, no train rides that I remember. There was no passage of time. And once we reached Mom's place, there was no standing outside the door, struggling for entrance. None of Mom's neighbors saw us come in. No one gave us a key. And no one has an explanation for these things, except CeCe and me, and ours isn't one Mom wants to hear.

Let's just say angels were involved. Did we see them?

No. But then, angels aren't in the habit of showing themselves. Besides, even if we had, even if we could describe them from head to toe, no one was prepared to believe us. Least of all Mom. This kind of stuff gives her the chills, which is sad because the truth is better than any tale we could whip up. In the end she took comfort in dismissing our account, calling it the product of a child's wild imagination, and deciding, unilaterally of course, that we were not to speak of "the incident" again.

I've kept it stored away in memory, along with all the other unexplained phenomena I've felt, or seen, or heard. I've got this idea, see, that God is saving me for something, that He's grooming me for a particular purpose in life, and all these spirit-world encounters are part of it somehow. If only I knew how the puzzle-pieces fit.

Shawna thinks I'm crazy for nursing this notion. Big surprise there! According to her, with the world being so big, and so desperately in need of help, what makes me think God has time to worry about saving me? For anything? Answers come hard, and Shawna's simply looking for an argument. I decide to give her neither. Besides, it's Sunday and I don't want to lie, not even to myself.

I don't know what God's got planned for me. Or why Dad had to die. Or why Mom can't quit drinking, or stay healthy, or figure out how to love me. I don't understand why CeCe and me got stuck with a life full of way too much drama. But I know if I've got questions, there must be answers.

One of these days I'm going to run into God, in a dream maybe, or in a vision, and I'm going to lay out all my questions, one at a time, and get the answers I need. And while I'm at it, I think I'll ask Him if there's really any connection between angels and UFOs.

. . .

*C*eCe came to school today. Mr. Sanders, our principal, called her in to talk about dress codes. He didn't like the African dress I wore this week, but his jaw really dropped when CeCe strode into his office, wrapped in yards of African fabric. Mr. Sanders forgot I was even there, he was so busy staring at her. He said something about how certain clothes can be a distraction in class, and then his voice trailed off.

CeCe eyed him for a minute, then said, "The next time you call me in, it had better be because Jazmin has broken the law, or is flunking a class. Otherwise, don't waste my time."

I bit my tongue to keep from laughing. I'd never watched anyone turn beet-red. Too bad I didn't have a camera.

CENTRAL PARK LESSON

Once, in Central Park
I slogged through
early morning mist
and grabbed a fistful
felt it lick
my fingers
then slip away,
rising, weightless
and invisible
to the sky
and all I
had left
to prove
its wet,
sun-silvered
reality
was the image
in my mind.

It seems to me that ideas are like gossamer, or mi fragile as a dream forgotten as soon as you awake. I gue that's why they're so hard to hold on to. But that's al what makes them wonderful, and more than worth the trouble.

I was in Central Park last Saturday when the idea f a poem sprinkled down on me, like a sudden showe and I knew it wouldn't last long.

I grabbed a pencil from behind my ear. I'd stuck there that morning when I'd done homework, and b was I glad. Panic set in, though, when I checked n pockets for paper. Wallet and keys were all I had on r because I'd gotten the notion from a kid at school th traveling light was cool.

No problem, I told myself, and went up to the fir stranger I could find to beg for a notebook page, or a na kin, or even a piece of tissue. But as soon as the lady sa me approach, she waved me away. Another woman tol me, flatly, that she didn't believe in handouts. Sever others eyed me suspiciously. Judging by the fear in the white faces, the fact that I was, at that moment, a franti wild-eyed, Black teenager probably had something to d with it. But who had time to dispel racial stereotypes

The poetry raining down on me was slowing to a trickle. If I didn't find writing paper soon, the poem would be lost.

I must've been quite a sight, though, staggering through the park in drab T-shirt and holey bell-bottoms, mumbling drunkenly, "Gotta find paper! Gotta find paper!" I was almost ready to give up when I spotted a garbage can, one of those open-grated kind the New York Parks Department seems to favor. I held my nose with one hand, and reached in with the other. It was pretty disgusting, I admit, but you do what you have to.

I carefully picked my way through crushed cans of Coke, balled up Kleenex, beer bottles, and old newspapers. Nothing I could use there. Then I got excited about two matchbook covers that were pretty clean, but they were too small for the job I had in mind.

Finally I found a crumpled, but otherwise unsullied, Hershey's candy bar wrapper, and whispered, *Thank God!* I ignored the passersby who wagged their heads as if to say "poor thing," squatted on the nearest curb, and scribbled like a maniac.

Here's the best part. I have no idea what that poem was about, or where that piece of paper is. It could have slipped from my pocket on the subway seat while the AA local lurched its way uptown. Or I could have dropped it in the stairwell when I ran up the three flights to our

apartment. Who knows. One way or another, I lost the poem by the time I got home that day, and I can't, for the life of me, recall a single verse. Nothing. Nada. Zilch.

But I do remember my fingers flying across that scrap of paper, and my heart pounding, and the rush I felt scratching out each word. I remember the excitement of molding that inspiration, and shaping it on the page, like clay. And I remember feeling powerful and powerless, all at once, and how the pleasure of that moment lingered for a long, long time. Even the remembering has joy in it. But the poem itself? Gone. Just . . . gone.

CeCe says everything happens in life to teach us something, and I believe her.

I'm not saying I completely understand the point of pouring your heart into a poem and then losing it forever. But from now on I'm carrying a pad and pen with me wherever I go. And I'm going to enjoy every good thing that comes my way, as much as I can, for as long as I can. I plan to treat each thing as if it's gossamer, or mist. Just in case.

NIGHT NOISE

Nightly bullet ricochets
remind me
that Death plays
hide-and-seek
round here.
Some consider it
a losing game.
But I clutch Hope's tail
and hold on tight.
For life, though tough at times,
is dear.

JULY 17

Death walks the streets around here by invitation. I try
to keep that fact from clogging up my mind, but that re-
quires the miraculous on a daily basis. I sure hope God's
supply of miracles holds out.

CeCe's old friend, Timothy, has given up on miracles

28

and snuggled up to Death since his return from Vietnam. At least once a week I find him nodding in our stairwell. It's mid-July, and yet his scrawny body swims in soiled gray sweats, smelling from two feet away. A faded blue jacket pretty much swallows up the top half of his body, except for his head, which I haven't seen him hold erect for months. He pockets his dirty syringe when he hears me coming, as if his slow suicide were a secret, but drugs have turned him into a brown ghost with flat black eyes, and anyone can see that he's itching for a burial. My question is, What's the rush?

CeCe and I spend all *our* time dodging bullets. A month ago, for instance, I was minding my own business, checking the mailbox in the vestibule, when a fight broke out in the street. I was near the door, but not in it, thank God, because a stream of bullets flew by too fast to count, and the line of fire was right about where my head would've been. Talk about a close call! Then, there was last night.

We had a poker party at our place to help raise cash. The usual players were there: Clyde from the record store. Goldy, who's got more yellow metal in his mouth than white enamel. Paulette, the redhead from the beauty shop, and the only woman wearing full makeup, including powder-blue eye shadow. Jolene, the light-skinned barmaid from The Garden of Eden, wearing her favorite platinum wig. (She owns at least three.) Crew, who, I swear, is really three men compressed into one body, although none of them have any hair to spare, judging by Crew's shiny black dome. And then, there was a first-timer named T.C. *Mmm, mmm, mmm* is the best way to describe him. He was a startling combination of dark and light, ebony skin and slate-gray eyes that had my heart singing "Ooo Baby Baby." His dreamy eyes reminded me of Smokey Robinson, the fine lead singer of Smokey Robinson and The Miracles. It's a wonder I didn't faint from love right there on the spot!

Crew was the only professional gambler. Nobody minded playing with him at our place, though, because he let everyone know that he was there for the fun, for the company. He gave his word, and that was plenty good enough. Besides, Crew is sweet on CeCe, and losing a couple of dollars to the house now and then is his way of getting in her good graces. Come to think of it, almost everyone was there to leave a small stack of cash on the table so that CeCe can pay the bills and have something left over for my school clothes, or shoes, or books, without having to go begging.

The card table was set up in the living room, but I

spent half the time in the kitchen frying up batches of chicken wings, and spooning out potato salad on paper plates. We do all right selling plates for a couple of dollars a pop. It's a great deal for the players, and adds to the silver in our piggy bank.

The kitchen is directly off the living room, so I could hear all the game noises. A sprinkle of laughter, the tap and shuffle of a crisp, freshly cut deck, the ching of coins piling up at the center of the table as players ante up, the tinkling of ice cubes melting in glasses of scotch and water, and Clyde, crude as ever, belching up beer. I could do without the last two sounds because I have no use for alcohol. But at least there wasn't much cussing to go along with the drinking, because CeCe won't have it. All in all, the game was quiet.

Crew ordered a plate of fried chicken. He's okay by me, so I gave him three extra wings, and a second dollop of potato salad. I set it down on the table beside him, and was about to turn, when Mr. Gray Eyes accused Crew of cheating, and whipped out a pistol. My eyes were glued to the gun barrel which, since I was inches away from Crew, was aimed in my general direction.

Fear bounced off the paint-chipped walls like a b-ball slamming a backboard. Nobody moved. Nobody breathed.

CeCe, bucking for an Oscar, said in a steely voice, "There will be no fighting in my house. If you want to kill each other, take it outside. Otherwise put that thing away and sit down." CeCe, who is all of five feet, one hundred five pounds soaking wet, stared T.C. down. "If there's going to be any shooting in here," she added evenly, "I'm going to be the one to do it." I swallowed hard and prayed in earnest then because, number one, CeCe cannot abide firearms and, number two, she doesn't own any.

T.C. studied my sister's face, decided she was not joking, and slowly put his piece away. All of a sudden it hit me why she's so good at poker. She knows how to bluff.

"I'm sorry," said T.C., taking his seat. "Sorry, man," he said to Crew. Crew, who has never cheated a day in his life, nodded stiffly, all the while memorizing this guy's face. Something tells me I wouldn't want to trade places with T.C.

Laughter returned to the room eventually, as if nothing major had happened, but that "nothing" followed me to bed and kept me awake for hours. Over and over again I shook my head, thinking how Death was at that table, in disguise, stalking CeCe and me in our own apartment. Thank God, last night, we walked away clean.

I don't want to be mean, but when I saw Timothy today, I had nothing to say to him. As far as I'm concerned, he can shoot poison in his veins and chase Death down all he wants to, but The Grim Reaper's gonna find me soon enough and, until he does, the only thing I'm chasing is tomorrow.

AUGUST

CeCe and I wait
in the welfare office
where the August heat
peels the paint
off the walls.
The caseworker
loosens his tie
curses the
unconditioned air
and shuffles papers
while we sweat
wondering if he'll decide
to help CeCe out
with extra money
now that my stay with her
is permanent.
I hate this waiting
but what really
makes me crazy
is all this man's talk

about the sin
of broken homes.
Inside I'm screaming
Don't you get it?
The homes
are just fine.
It's the people
who are broken.

I t's the first day of school, and once again I'm the secondhand queen. I shuffle into class, with my head down, awkward in my mustard blouse and knee-length khaki skirt. Last year's colors. Last year's style. I pray no one notices, but fear the worst.

"There's nothing wrong with clothes that are secondhand," my grandmother loves to say, "as long as their design is first rate." To prove it, she marches me downtown to the garment district every now and then for her own version of Fashion 101. We'll go into an outlet that sells some European fashion designer whose name I can't pronounce, and she'll point out hand-stitching, and discuss the drape, and the cut, and the quality of the fabric. So, thanks to her, I fully understand the pedigree of my recycled skirts and jackets. I know that all my clothes are well-made, each seam smartly double-stitched, with the finest craftsmanship. Ya-da, ya-da, ya-da.

Well, that's great. But my skin aches for the feel of never-worn lamb's wool sweaters, or brushed suede, or even plain blue-jean jackets—so long as they're straight off the department store rack. I try them on sometimes. But I'm quick to put them back once I hear CeCe's voice in my head, loud and clear, saying, "Jazmin, you know we don't have that kind of money."

My classmate Chavonne Honeywood doesn't have that problem. My question is, Why do girls with names that sound smooth as a 100-dollar bill always seem to have what I want? It's not as though they deserve it more than me. After all, God don't like ugly, and it is sheer meanness the way Chavonne and her friends look down their noses at everybody. They're fashion pirates who parade through the school halls in bright-colored minis, and thigh-high lizard boots, with a treasure-chest full of silver bracelets jingling along the length of their skinny arms, and I hate it. They get all the cute clothes, and all the cute boys, and there's nothing fair about it.

I won't admit to being crazy-jealous. Not to them. But

Alexander's department store barely missed being the scene of a crime the last time I went shopping, and temporary insanity was definitely involved.

Black tights was all I was looking for, but Hosiery was next to Shoes, and a few yards beyond that was my favorite department. I can see it now, the neon lights flashing "57th Street," the section where they keep the latest, and most expensive, styles for teens. Looking was my first mistake. From that point on, my body was taken over by an alien.

It was somebody else who passed through the narrow entryway of "57th Street," someone else who drooled over clothes that smelled of money, someone else who floated into the dressing room to try on a dress so red, it burned her fingers. Once I was in front of the mirror, though, I had to admit, that someone was me. And, naturally, since I couldn't afford the dress, it was a perfect fit.

I turned my back to the security camera, neatly folded the silky soft, double-knit mini into my oversized canvas shoulder bag. Then I stood at the dressing room door for about an eon or two, waiting for the good sense God gave me to return. It never did. But luckily, fear took over. The thought of being caught and sent to prison for shoplifting made me wet my pants, so I hung the dress back where it belonged, and ran out of the store. I've been going over that scene in my head ever since.

I still want that red dress. I think of it sometimes when I see Chavonne. I'm convinced she hangs around the school entrance longer than necessary, to pose in her new clothes, to torture me. And it works too. But that's okay. One day I'll have enough money to buy my clothes off the rack.

Meanwhile I've got more brains and talent in my pinky than Chavonne has in her whole body, and I'm not looking to trade places. Just clothes.

I thought high school guidance counselors were supposed to help keep students on track, but last week mine tried putting me on a train going in the opposite direction altogether. Her name is Lillian Wise. She takes the meaning too much to heart, if you ask me. I didn't realize that until I got my course schedule for next term, signed by her, which was filled with courses I'd never choose. Home economics was one. General science was another. There was no chemistry, no French or Spanish, but sewing for beginners was included in the schedule. Not exactly the kind of courses I need to get into college.

I went directly to her office to ask how this obvious mistake had occurred. Her desk, with its neatly organized stacks of papers and student file folders, gave me a clue. Everything seemed in its proper place, which is where she thought to put me. "My experience," she said, "tells me that a person like yourself would be happier in the business world. Or maybe doing something with your hands."

"A person like myself," I repeated. "What exactly does that mean?" I didn't honestly expect an answer, so her silence came as no surprise. At this point, though, I was tempted to search her office for mammy dolls.

I planted myself in front of Miss Wise's desk and started counting. Ten. Nine. Eight. Seven. Images of stimulating talks at the college snack bar, discussing politics and God and the state of the state, flash before my eyes. I have visions of sheepskin diplomas, and gold-tassled, three-cornered graduation caps and gowns. Dreams of escaping The Garden of Eden and poker parties, Amsterdam Avenue and days of making do rush by. I see myself dazzling university professors with my perfectly articulated Black brilliance. I'm an A-student, so it's not as if I were completely delusional. And then it hits me: All this could be blasted away by the strategically placed bias of one Miss Lillian Wise, who stares at me and casually asks, "What seems to be the problem?"

But I was cool. Downright cold, in fact. Think dry ice.

"Miss Wise," I said, my voice a whisper, "I'd appreciate it if you'd revise my course schedule immediately, as I have every intention of going to college."

"Well," she said, huffiness personified, "I was simply trying to help."

I stared at her for a minute, my eyes, twin suns, burning through my magnified eyeglass lenses. "Well, Miss Wise," I said as she fanned herself, "don't." I banged her door on my way out.

I could've told CeCe what happened when I got home that day, but I decided the apartment was too tiny to contain both my outrage and hers. I'll tell her one of these days, I suppose. In a year maybe.

There's not much you can do about a person like Miss Wise, except to be glad that not everyone in the world is half as bad as she. My English teacher, Mrs. Vogel, who did double-duty as my guidance counselor last year, couldn't be more different. She nudges me toward Shakespeare, and slips copies of novels by James Baldwin and Gwendolyn Brooks in my book bag when she thinks I'm not looking.

I stopped by her homeroom this morning to say

hello, and was rewarded by her smile. She wanted to know how my classes were going, and asked about Mom's recovery, as she often does.

"You need to see her, Jazmin," she said, her eyes holding mine. "It's time. No matter what she's done, she's your mother. Remember that." *Yeah, well,* I thought, *somebody should've told Mom that before she shipped me off to my first foster home.* Still, I know Mrs. Vogel was right.

"If you need an ear," said Mrs. Vogel, "you know where to find me." I've talked with her before about my problems at home, past and present, and about Mom. I don't remember half the things I say. There's so much anger mixed in with my words, clear thoughts and muddied feelings are impossible to separate. But Mrs. Vogel's a great listener. She lets me let off steam.

We talk awhile, discuss the finer points of studying Spanish over German, and weigh the usefulness of French in my future study of English literature. She points out the payoff of pounding my head against the brick wall of geometry, and higher mathematics. And she says, "Jazmin, I'll be very disappointed if you don't do great things with your life. You've got real talent. Don't waste it." Then we hug, and I go to my next class.

41

I've been assigned two different counselors so far, Miss Wise and Mrs. Vogel, and between the two, I know whose advice I'm taking.

•   •   •   •

Today was my birthday. I'm glad it fell on a Saturday this year, so I could concentrate on me. Birthdays should be personal holidays anyway.

No card from Mom. Not that I expected one. She's so out of it, I wonder if she'll remember her own birthday this year. Still, I was hoping....

I wish I could have a normal birthday, where Mom throws me a surprise party and everybody sings "Happy Birthday" off-key. But I guess I'm just being silly.

CeCe bought me the cutest radio. It looks like a miniature TV. We saw it in a store window. I drooled over it, then sighed loud enough for CeCe to hear. She told me not to bat my big eyes at her, which I did immediately, so I knew she'd put the radio on layaway. CeCe's such a pushover.

Happy Birthday to me!

DAYDREAMING

Yesterday
I visited my favorite spot
at Macombs Park
three blocks away.
I crept as far down the bank
as my leather loafers
would let me
without slipping
then I pulled up
a slab of rock
and sat beside
the Harlem River.
I couldn't see
the mouth of the river
from where I sat
but I could hear it talking.
It told me I'd be
a famous author someday
that my arm'll be worn out
from signing autographs
everywhere I go.

and my fans will beg me
to name the characters
in my next book
after them.
I'll smile
promising nothing
and say
"I'll keep that in mind."
Which just goes to show
that even though
the Harlem
is not as old
as the Nile
it'll do
for dreaming.

*M*iss Warren, the high school art teacher-slash-sculptor, has been rhapsodizing about my profile for a week now. What is with her? She says my profile has "character," but even a child knows that character is what you want to *have*, not how you want to *look*. I'm usually referred to as cute-without-the-glasses, and that's exactly the way it's said, run together, as if it's all one word. I despise the description, ordinarily—however, even that sounds attractive by comparision. But who am I kidding. There's nothing cute about my hooked nose. Mom's got one too, so I know who to thank, especially since nobody else in my family has been blessed with this noble feature. I've formed a theory to explain its origin.

"I must have Jewish blood in me," I tell my friend Sophie. Sophie's skin is thin and white as the fine china bowl CeCe found on one of her secondhand store shopping binges. Sophie's hair and lashes are black as mine, but that's our only real resemblance. Except for the round, nonprescription granny glasses she wears for show, something I'll never understand.

We were taking a breather in the gym locker room after P.E. I studied my nose in the mirror on the locker door. I tried willing it to shrink, but no luck.

"I'm telling you, I must be from one of the Lost Tribes. How else can you account for my hooked nose?" I say.

Sophie turns her startling blue-gray eyes on me, cracks a smile, but just barely, and says, without missing a beat, "Then maybe you should think about getting a nose job."

Sophie's quick, which is precisely why we're such good friends.

"Seriously," I say. "There's something *to* this. For instance, how many Black people you know can sing "Hava Nagila," hmm? What about my propensity for guilt? And let's not *even get* into how wild I am for *knish*!" Sophie turns her silky black brows into question marks, and shakes her head.

"You are hopeless."

Sophie knows I love her, and never takes offense.

All jokes aside, I honestly believe Jews and Blacks have a lot in common. We're both familiar with ghettoes, and we both know about discrimination, that's for sure. And when it comes down to it, pain is pain. Doesn't anybody get that, besides me? Besides Sophie?

My mom's best friend, Esther, is a Black Jew. She converted when she got married, I think. I remember going to the celebration of her son's bar mitzvah, and suddenly being an alien, lost in a sea of yarmulked men, and beautiful women hiding their beautiful hair under plainwoven scarves. And the food! Everything was delicious, but I couldn't wrap my tongue around the names of half the things I ate. Mom could, though. She seemed at home with it all, seemed to fit right in. She even tried out Judaism for a while. She brought home a Jewish prayer book once, CeCe says, and she studied books on Hebrew grammar. She was pretty serious about converting at one point. Her temple days didn't last long, though, but her

46

friendship with Esther did. Will my friendship with Sophie?

"How is she, by the way? Your mom, I mean."

"How do you *do* that?" I asked Sophie. That child is forever reading my mind. "She's okay, I guess."

"You still haven't been to see her. Chicken."

What if I go and see her and start crying? Or what if she looks through me as if I'm not there? Am I supposed to act like I don't care? God, I wish I didn't!

I shook my head and looked down at the floor, thinking, *Sophie, I really don't want to get into this now.* Fortunately for me, the school bell rang.

"Oh, joy!" I said. "Math!"

"Here," said Sophie, handing me a record. I looked down and smiled at the title: *How Sweet It Is (To Be Loved By You)*, by Marvin Gaye. I loaned her the 45 a week ago. She's got eyes and ears for John Lennon alone, and I'm trying to broaden her musical field of vision, but these things take time.

"Listen, Jaz. A bunch of us are going out for fish-'n'-chips at lunch. Want to come?"

"I wish," I groaned. "I'm brown-bagging it."

"Knowing your sister, I'll bet it's something gourmet."

"Not exactly," I said. Then I hit her with the gory details.

47

Money is scarce in our house at the moment, but have no fear! CeCe's favorite supermarket has a sale on eggs. Lucky me!

Let's see, so far this week, we've had scrambled eggs, poached eggs, deviled eggs, eggs and grits, eggs and hash browns, egg salad, and, for an exotic change of pace, eggs Benedict! The French toast was a tasty twist. And lest I forget, last night we dined on egg-drop soup. Whoop-di-do!

"CeCe may be a wonderful cook," I said to Sophie, "but geez-Louise! I used to think the Israelites were pretty ungrateful, griping to God about all that manna.

"There they are after the Exodus, wandering in the desert with no food, and *Boom!* God sends them some. Okay, so it wasn't exactly pizza. It was more like oatmeal maybe, or grain for baking bread—something without a lot of taste. Even so, how many people are lucky enough to get food from heaven every day? And for free? But all they could think about were the leeks and onions back in Egypt.

"Well, I finally understand. The manna was probably fine—for the first two or three days. But after a while you start thinking, No offense, God, but I wouldn't mind liver and onions right about now. The change would do me good."

Suddenly there was this sly twinkle in Sophie's blue eyes that wasn't there a second ago. "Oh! I almost forgot!

My mom said to invite you over tonight," she dead-panned. "We're having *omelettes*."

Then Sophie threw her head back, and laughed.

I didn't expect to start losing brain cells until I turned 30, but I must be getting an early jump on it because I ditched school today for no other reason than to be able to say I did. And I happen to *love* school. Not the rules, of course, or the mystery meat served in the cafeteria, but finding out about other centuries, other cultures in far-off places, discovering new ways to stretch my mind, and reading, which I can't get enough of—those things I love. What I hate is being called "geek" and "Goody Two-shoes" because every kid I know has skipped at least a day at school, except for me. Until today.

CeCe has this annoying saying she frequently tortures me with, ostensibly to make me think. "If everybody jumps off a bridge," she says, "will you jump too?" Then I answer on cue, "What's that got to do with anything?" And I wave her off, amazed that she sometimes forgets I'm smart enough to know my own mind.

49

My best friend, Destinee, was my partner-in-crime for the day. We rendezvoused in the school yard near the basketball court, not hiding in the shadows, but in plain sight. After all, unless you risk being caught, ditching school loses a degree of its appeal. Having fulfilled this unwritten rule, we ducked out like the thieves we were, stealing time, and flew to the corner bus stop without letting our feet touch the ground.

We headed downtown to the projects on Madison where Wardell, a boy in my history class, had a cousin, who had a neighbor named Carlton, a guy in his twenties, who's usually home—I don't ask why—and who likes having kids around. Destinee and I hardly know the kids who hang out there, since we've never been before, whereas the other kids are regulars.

I knocked on Carlton's zinc-plated door, the one smooth thing his apartment had going for it. His living room was a disaster of dirty dishes, empty pizza boxes, candy wrappers, crushed soda cans, and wrinkled clothing flung over chair arms, Lava lamps, or wherever else there happened to be space. An unmade sofa bed stood in the center of the room. No one seemed to notice the messiness, though. The haze of burning incense, hashish, and marijuana probably clouded their vision.

So much for Carlton's apartment. As for the man, that's another story. He was luscious looking and impossible to miss, which explained why the girls in the place outnumbered the guys. He was a six-foot-four chocolate drop with hazel eyes, and a bush of wavy hair that grazed his shoulders and reminded me so much of a lion's mane, I half expected him to growl.

Carlton gave Destinee the once-over, which was no surprise. She's got high cheekbones, a wide, flat nose, huge hazel eyes, and she fills out a sweater better than most girls, but it's her height people notice. She's five-foot-nine and all legs, born to race, or pirouette across a stage, or model women's stockings, something that re-quires showing off the feature that guarantees her whis-tles wherever she goes. Her long, dark caramel legs end in long, narrow feet she considers an embarrassment, but she'd look ridiculous with tiny feet, and I've told her as much. I'd be jealous of her good looks, if she wasn't my best friend. I was just glad that, when Carlton finished checking her out, he turned his gorgeous eyes on me.

I managed to look away from him long enough to no-tice that there were kids, wall-to-wall, spread out on the area rug, draped on the arms of the sofa, and lazing on the love seat in front of the gated window. Destinee and I joined the circle on the floor.

A tight knot of kids in the corner shared squares of aluminum foil covered with sprinklings of white powder. From the way they were snorting it, I knew it wasn't talcum. And I noticed Carlton pop a couple of pills and swallow them down with a glass of sangria. But everybody else stuck to drinking wine and smoking grass. The good stuff, they said. Colombian. What is Colombian anyway? As soon as I sat, the joint was passed to me. *What the hell*, I thought. *This is grass, not cocaine. Once won't kill me.* I took a drag and held it in as long as I could, imitating everyone around me. Then I passed it to Destinee.

I'm not sure when it hit me, but I distinctly recall surrendering to a bout of giggles, for who knows what reason, then wanting salt one minute and craving sweets the next. And when I tried standing, my legs were suddenly brown licorice sticks, bending every which way. I staggered to the bathroom, and when I got there, I saw a stranger in the mirror who had my face, except that her eyes were slits, and her other features seemed blurry. *God*, I thought, *if CeCe saw me now!*

I asked Carlton if there was somewhere I could lie down for a while, and he waved me to a back bedroom. *If I rest for a minute*, I told myself, *I'll be fine.* So I curled up on the bed and closed my eyes.

I don't know how long I slept, but I woke to the feel of another person's weight pressed against me, and a hand traveling to places on my body marked no trespassing, and I was sure it was there without invitation. My eyes flew open and I rolled over to find Carlton staring back at me. Suddenly it occurs to me why he likes having kids around. Especially girls. He's cute, I admit, and I wouldn't mind taking his lips for a test run one day maybe. But not today. I shoved him hard to let him know it'd be wise for him to quit while he was ahead, but all he did was lick his lips and reach for me again.

"Come on, baby," he said, his voice husky. "I won't hurt you. I just want to get close to you. Don't you want to feel close?"

I was close to the wall, I know that. As a matter of fact, I tried pressing myself into it. "Now look, Carlton," I said, "let me lie here for a while and rest, okay? That's all I'm asking."

Carlton inched closer, apparently hard of hearing.

I clenched my teeth, starting to fume, more mad at me than him, since being there was my bright idea, not his. *What's wrong with you, Jazmin?* I asked myself. *What are you doing here?* My brain was way too fuzzy to form an answer. That grass had me half in, half out of my head, and I could hardly think straight, which I hated. I always try to be clear in my mind about everything I do, good or bad. That way, later on I can say I know I did it on purpose.

Carlton shoved a knee between my legs and pulled me to him. I tensed up, especially when I heard the moans coming from down the hall. I know those sounds. I hear them at school sometimes when I pass close to a guy feeling up his girlfriend in the shadow of the stairwell. And at parties where the parents are away, and couples slip off to a back bedroom when no one's looking so they can crawl all over each other in private. *I'm not ready for this*, I thought. *I know that much.*

Roughly 200 pounds of flesh and bone, named Carlton, separated me from the bedroom door. I gave that serious consideration, then I relaxed in Carlton's arms. I let him hold me for a minute, forced myself to breathe evenly. When his grip on me loosened, I looked up and grinned, rubbing the sturdy muscles of his arm. "You like those muscles, don't you?" he bragged. I nodded, and murmured with mock appreciation. Then I started wiggling around.

"Ooooh! Oh, man," I said. "I gotta go. That 7Up must be kicking in. Where's your bathroom?"

"Down the hall," he said. "But don't stay too long."

"I won't," I said, still smiling. "Keep my place warm." Then I climbed over him. Not too fast, not too slow. I grabbed my glasses from the nightstand, slipped on my sneakers, and double-timed it to the front door. Thank God the bathroom was in the same direction.

I had a tough time navigating between the legs and feet of all the kids spread out across the living room rug, some kissing hot and heavy, others dozing. Destinee was one of the latter. I shook her awake. "I'm outta here," I said. "You can stay if you want to." Destinee rubbed her eyes and staggered to her feet.

"Wait up," she said. "I'm right behind you."

The cool, late-afternoon air helped sober me, and by the time we got to the bus stop, I knew I didn't care how geeky anybody thought I was. "Destinee," I said. "Remind me not to do this again."

There's no way she could've understood all I meant by "this," but Destinee's a good friend, so she nodded and said, "You got it."

UNTITLED

Got a letter
from Mom today
but couldn't read
her chicken scratches.
CeCe says
Mom's medication
makes her hand shake.
No matter.
I'd rather not
decipher the message
just now.
Mom means well
but her words
are no help
when kids at school
give me
the usual quiz:
"How come you live
with your sister?
How come you don't

live with your mom?"
What am I
supposed to say?
My mom's away.
Not just her body
but her mind.
Where does she go?
      How should I know?

Some people have no business being parents, legal age notwithstanding. I wish someone would tell them that.

My classmate Shawna is nine months pregnant with a belly to prove it, and everyone is quick to say she's way too young to be a mother. No argument there. Not even from Shawna, who is less than thrilled with the prospect, especially since the boy who helped get her into the family way immediately helped himself to a bus ticket out of Dodge. When anyone asks, "Whatever happened to Tariq?" his mother says, "Tariq went to stay with his father for a while." Then underneath her breath she mutters, "I am not about to have that boy bringing no babies into my house!" Shawna's own mom threatened to throw her out, though Mrs. Marcus has finally come around and agreed to give her daughter a hand now that the baby is almost here. So.

But it's not only kids my age who should stay away from parenting. Lisann Ramsey, who just turned 30, was so busy flirting with J.D., who was posturing in front of The Garden this afternoon, that she failed to notice Deyona, her two year old, toddling off the curb and into traffic. I ran to the corner, grabbed that sweetie by her denim jumper strap, and scooped her up. She giggled, figuring that we were playing airplane, and having no idea whatsoever that I'd probably saved her life. I finger-combed her tight red curls, made sure she was okay, then took her over to her mother.

"You might try keeping your eye on your daughter," I snapped. Lisann snatched Deyona from my arms.

The girl was decked out in an electric-blue hot-pants suit, silk no less, and who wears silk hot-pants on a weekday, in the middle of the afternoon, to take a baby out for fresh air? No one, which is why I shouldn't have been surprised when Lisann went right back to batting those silly lashes of hers. But not before she cut her eyes at me to let me know she didn't much appreciate having her flirtation interrupted.

This is exactly the kind of thing that makes me wonder if mothering is all in the genes. Take Destinee's mom. Children are first with her—her kids, and everybody else's. She gathers me up in her arms as if those arms were made for hugging, and I'm not even her child. Yet this seems to be no strain on her affections. She makes time to talk, to listen, to kid around with me, and this all comes naturally.

My mom, on the other hand, is not strong on communication, or affection. She never was. When CeCe and I were little, she'd pull away from our hugs as if they made her uncomfortable. Grandma was the same way, but CeCe and I hug our friends and each other all the time, so maybe the need skipped a couple of generations.

Mom often preferred work to home. She never said so, but it's pretty hard to miss. While Destinee's mom itches to get home from her job every day, so she can spend time with her family, Mom is the first to raise her hand when her boss wants volunteers to work overtime. Overtime, double-time, time and a half—if you want her, she's there. Meanwhile, I had to get used to checking my own homework and eating meals alone. She said we needed the extra money, and that might've been partly true, but it didn't explain how relieved she was to be anywhere but home. Unless there was a man around, and that usually spelled trouble.

Most of the men Mom brought home had a tendency to lick their lips and leer at me when they thought she wasn't looking, which I hated. And sooner or later they'd encourage her to drink, which I hated even more. The appearance of alcoholic beverages in the house generally signalled the beginning of a downward spiral I was painfully familiar with. First would come the casual drinking, then the serious binges, where Mom would take off for days at a time. Eventually the pressure of trying to work in an alcoholic haze would push her toward a complete nervous breakdown. When she'd start talking about hearing voices, or whispering about strangers spying on her day and night, I'd call Grandma and say, "It's time." And someone from Bellevue Hospital would come to take Mom away.

I'd seen the pattern so often, I could mark its stages. So why couldn't I do anything to stop it? It's a question I often ask.

While Mom was away, I'd be shunted off to an aunt, or a cousin, or to foster care. It all depended on who was willing to make room for me the longest, because Mom's hospitalization usually ran up to three months. Which pretty much left Daddy out of the picture.

Daddy was tender, and gentle, and loved CeCe and me so much, sometimes he looked as if he'd burst. He spent as much time with us as he could, when Mom didn't keep him at a distance, that is. But he never felt qualified to raise kids on his own. When we were young, a week or two of bunking with him in Brooklyn, scrunched up on his sofa (neither of us liked his lumpy bed) was all we could ever count on from him. CeCe and I are too old for that these days. Besides, Daddy's gone now, so we don't even have that.

CeCe gave up on Mom being a there-for-you kind of mother long ago, and moved out when she was sixteen. She lived with a guy for a while, until she could find a job waitressing, save up salary and tips, and get her own place. Then, soon as she was settled, she said, "Jazmin, you've got a place with me if you want it. When you're ready, say the word." The last time Mom surrendered to alcohol and a nervous breakdown, I took CeCe up on her offer.

CeCe is convinced that she's my real mom anyway, which is kind of funny since there's barely six years between us. She often took care of me when I was in diapers, she says. She's got no proof, but considering how she fusses over me, and has a heart attack if I come home late without calling, I'm prepared to take her word for it. But I do wish I could get her to quit referring to me as her "baby," especially in front of my friends. *There are worse things*, I keep telling myself. *Like having nobody love you.*

I'll say one thing, though. I'm in no hurry to have kids. It's obvious that marriage is risky business, and I refuse to put a kid of mine through the hell of divorce and foster care, and all the rest. I'm not saying I'll never get married, or that I will, only that I'll take my own sweet time, find someone who's ready to go the distance.

Meanwhile, I'll try a baby-sitting job, see how that goes. It's not the same as being a full-time mom, of course, but maybe it can help me figure out if I have the parenting instinct. That sort of thing might be hereditary, and if I'm missing that particular gene, I'd rather find out in advance.

● ● ● ●

OCTOBER 25

I ran into Aunt Sarah on her way from the beauty parlor yesterday, her hot-curled silver hair gleaming with coconut oil and plenty of style. She took one look at my unruly strands and said, "Child, it's time for you to do something with that head of yours." My mirror told me

62

she was right. After dinner I called Destinee to see if her father, who owns Bill's Barber and Style on Amsterdam Avenue, was home. His name isn't Bill, it's Abraham, but it seems the place has been called Bill's for as long as anyone can remember. Abraham—Mr. Joysmith, that is—was home, and told me to come right over.

I may be a girl, but I don't see much point in going to the beauty salon, considering the way I wear my hair these days. Besides, Mr. Joysmith cuts my hair for free. He says he needs the practice. Right. Am I supposed to believe he's suddenly going to get a run of ladies who wear naturals, crowding into his barbershop for haircuts? I don't think so. It's more like he knows that *free* is the only kind of haircut I can afford. Not that I'd pay him, even if I could.

Yesterday he did his usual. He sat me in a chair in the middle of his living room, wrapped a towel around my shoulders to protect my shirt, and laid out the spare clippers he keeps at home. Then he begins the ritual. "So, how do you want your hair cut today?" he asks.

"A little shaggy in the back," I tell him, "short on the sides, and a little longer on top and in front."

"Okay," he says, nodding. He switches on the clippers, tilts my head back, and says, "Let's see what we can do." Then he proceeds to cut my hair one-inch thick all over, front, back, and sides, as if I'd never said a word. It's the same routine every time.

I believe my teachers at school would call that an inability to follow instructions. Fortunately I don't mind too much. I like to keep my hair short and simple.

Miriam Makeba is the one to thank for that. She proved there can be a connection between short, natural hair and Black beauty. Daddy used to talk about her, and her South African music. He had an entire collection of her records. And he had pictures of her, and other African women, on album covers, and book jackets, and posters plastered on the walls of his apartment.

My father loved Miriam Makeba. And it wasn't the music alone.

If Daddy were alive, that's one thing he and Mr. Joysmith would have in common: finding Miriam Makeba beautiful, and believing that, when I wear my hair like hers, I am too. So, after giving it careful consideration, I've decided to adopt Destinee's dad as my honorary second father. I doubt he'll have any objections, but for now I'll keep the information to myself.

A girl can't be too careful.

I do wish he'd cut my hair on top with less enthusiasm, though. And he could leave enough in the back for me to grab hold of. But free is free, and you have to make exceptions for fathers who mean well.

I tried writing Mom last night, but it was no use. What am I supposed to say? I miss you? I've been missing her half my life. Hope you're feeling better? Half of me hopes she does, but the other half keeps thinking, *Serves you right, choosing booze over CeCe and me.* But that hospital can't be much fun, and I do feel sorry for Mom, mostly. I'll wait a couple of days. Maybe I can come up with a few lines then.

YARDBIRD SUITE

I heard Daddy last night
wailing on his sax.
The notes were so blue and sweet
I shook myself awake
and danced into the living room
for a better listen.
But it was only CeCe,
playing Charlie Parker
on the stereo.
Daddy loved him some
Charlie Parker.

NOVEMBER 7
━━━━

I could ask CeCe's friend Crew where he got his name, but judging from his bulk, I'm betting it comes from "crew," as in wrecking. Now there's a name to inspire fear, and fear's something I know about. It finds me in the dark.

Last Saturday CeCe ran out of cigarettes late at night

and sent me down to The Garden of Eden to get a pack from their machine. She was in her nightgown, and I was still dressed, so it made sense that I should be the one to go. CeCe doesn't want me smoking, yet there she was sending me out to buy her a pack of menthols. Talk about a hypocrite!

Anyway, CeCe warned me not to dawdle, then called the bartender to say I was on the way, and to ask him to keep an eye out for me.

"Watch out for ghouls," said CeCe, walking me to the door.

"Check the calendar," I shot back. "Halloween was five days ago." I slipped my jacket on and headed downstairs.

I was in and out of The Garden in maybe five minutes. The Avenue, silent as a Sunday morning, felt downright creepy at 10:30 P.M. The broken street lamp didn't help. Is there such a thing as double darkness? I don't know, but I felt as though I was slogging my way through shadow thick as three feet of snow in December. I walked as fast as I could, eyes darting left and right. CeCe says, in this town it pays to be paranoid, and I happen to agree.

"Hey, sugar," said a deep voice, startling me. The man who owned it oozed from a dark doorway, all oily skin, and slick hair, and snakeskin shoes. I never felt him there, never heard a sound. He was nice looking and well dressed, which must be why he thought he'd get somewhere with me. Whoever he was.

He tried to block my path, but I sidestepped him and sucked my teeth as if to say, Man, you are wasting your time. Meanwhile, I made sure to pick up my pace.

"Whatcha doin' out here, all by yo' sweet self? Come here," he said, staggering close enough for his 40-proof breath to ferment the air around me.

Leave me alone, my brain was screaming. I stuffed my hands into my pockets, acting tough to disguise how badly I was shaking, and felt around for my keys, in case I suddenly needed something sharp. The man grabbed a handful of my jacket from behind, and pulled. My legs turned to blocks of ice.

"Chase! You got a problem I can help you with?" said a voice. I looked around, but didn't see anyone. The voice belonged to a man, though, and it sounded near. Chase looked around too, suddenly jumpy. He didn't seem to know where the voice came from either, but it was clear the sound of it made him agitated.

"Uh, no problem, man," he said. "I was just—"

"You were just going on about your business."

"Uh, right," said Chase. And he moved on down the street.

Me, I'm still frozen in place, because all I see ahead of

me is darkness, and I'm wondering who and where this other man is, because maybe he wants me for himself. I swallow hard and tell my feet to pretend they've got good sense, and to get going, which they finally do. I'm nearly home free, six steps shy of the stoop. *Thank God,* I say to no one. Then a beefy hand settles on my shoulder.

"You okay, Jaz?" I turn, clearly able to make out the face from the light in the Laundromat. It was Crew, a menacing sight in black shirt, black slacks, black jacket, black hat, and wire-rim shades. Lord, was I glad to see him!

"That was you?" I asked. "Where were you?"

Crew flashed a mouthful of gold at me, but did not answer. "Go on inside," he said. "I'll watch you from here."

I thanked him and bounded up the stairs, shaking my head, thinking, *Crew to the rescue. Imagine.*

Now that's what I call a guardian angel out of uniform.

• • •

*C*eCe and I have never shopped for a pet, but that doesn't mean we're minus furry visitors, even if they are unwanted.

Last night an oily black one, tail long as a leather whip curled at the tip, ambled through my room. The scratch of his jagged claws woke me in time to return his beady-eyed stare. I shivered during his sharp appraisal, and wondered if other members of his clan waited nearby. I was not particularly keen on having my fingers and toes serve as his family's late-night snack.

The main thing, I told myself, *is to lie still and pretend to be fearless.*

Eventually Mr. Rat continued his rounds, swaggering on into the living room where, thankfully, the hair-raising scratch of his claws was muffled by the carpeting. Once it was safe, I slipped my bare feet over the side of the sofa bed, and ran into CeCe's room to rouse her. If I was spending the night wide-eyed and sleepless, worrying about Mr. Rat's return, then CeCe was keeping me company.

Share and share alike, I say.

CeCe hates rats less fiercely than I, but when I mentioned our furry visitor, she leapt out of bed, sprinted to the kitchen, and—went straight to the fridge. She filled a jelly jar with Coke, and offered me a drink. I shrugged, took several sips, and waited for her to explain what rats and cola have to do with one another. She winked at me, wrapped the empty soda bottle in a brown grocery bag, and smashed it against the kitchen sink. Then she marched to the living room, bent down by the radiator, and lifted the flap of carpet in front of it.

"There!" she said, pointing to a gash in the floor. "I thought that's where that devil was sneaking in. But I bet I know how to put an end to that!"

Immediately CeCe began plugging the ugly cavity with bits of broken glass. When I saw what she was up to, I gave her a hand.

"I saw a rat the other day," said CeCe, stuffing the last Coke-bottle shard into the hole. "It was probably the same one you saw. Lord, it was big! About the size of a kitten, similar to the ones we had over on Lenox. You were too young to remember, but at night Mama used to put you in the top dresser drawer so the rats couldn't reach you, 'cause they never could resist the sweet smell of milk on a baby's breath."

"Oh, thanks, CeCe!" I groaned. "That was a *big* help!"

Now I'm really shivering, and wondering why CeCe

chose that particular moment to share that particular story. Between her remembered rats and my real one, sleep couldn't have found me with a searchlight.

I went back to bed and laid there, stiff enough to fool an undertaker, my eyes pried open by fear, for who knows how long. I tried willing my muscles to relax, but every time they started to, the image of that disease-ridden rodent crept across the screen of my mind, and I tensed up all over again.

Take your mind off of it, I told myself. So I imagined myself packing up boxes of books, and clothes, and dishes, and then stacking them inside a moving van. I'm driving downtown. Next thing I know, I'm unloading those cartons in front of a brownstone, or maybe a condo, across from Central Park. A man in a brass-buttoned uniform with gold braid at the shoulders, props the door open for me. I pause in the entryway and smile, because this place is new, and clean, with no smells of wine or urine in the halls. This place is distinctly devoid of rats and roaches. But especially rats.

And then I see myself waltzing in and out of fancy galleries on Madison, turning a discriminating eye on the high-priced paintings and sculptures—money is no object, which is why this is called a dream—and I'm slinky in purple silk, with silver bracelets running up and down my arms, and my purse is bulging with hundred-dollar bills.

Then I figure, *Wait a minute. I've got a better idea.*

I see myself strolling along the Champs Élysées in Paris, and pausing at one of those sidewalk cafes, where I join James Baldwin, my favorite author, for a short chat, and then I'm tossing coins in Rome's Fontana di Trevi to make a wish, and suddenly I realize that, by being there, my wish has already been granted.

Then the scene changes. I'm lying on the beach of Saint Croix, or stretched out on a blanket somewhere along the coast of the Red Sea, in East Africa. I'm brown and beautiful in white shorts and shirt, and sunglasses, not eyeglasses, because, miraculously, I've got 20-20 vision. I have a notebook in hand, white sand is tickling my toes, and I'm jotting down notes for the Great American Novel.

I squint up at the midday sun, decide to take a breather, and grab a mango from my picnic basket. I sink my teeth into its tart sweetness, then lick the juice that gathers in the corners of my mouth, certain that I've never tasted anything so delicious! I'm about to take a second bite when, wouldn't you know it, a sand crab, hoping for scraps, scuttles by. Something about that beady-eyed crab seems familiar, and why does it have a tail? I don't know, because my mind is swirling, and I can't get a fix on much of anything now, so I finally drift off to sleep.

The next morning CeCe told me I have a wonderful imagination. "Well," I said, "it comes in handy. But, you know, we really should think about getting a cat."

*B*renda got on my last nerve at school today. She elbowed me on the stairs, made me lose my balance, then dared me to do something about it. She's been pushing me around for weeks, and I've tried to ignore it. Brenda doesn't know this, but nasty tempers run in my family, and I really don't want to explode all over her. I thought I'd stuff my anger until she finally got bored trying to rile me, and found someone else to pick on to get her kicks. But who was I kidding? Holding things in is what made my mom crazy, and even if my plan had worked, I'd still have all that mad bubbling up in me, and that's no good. I decided to let it out instead.

I ran down the hall after Brenda, spun her around, and shoved her against a wall, blocking her body with my own. She's got 20 pounds on me, but anger multiplied my muscle. "Look," I said in a dead whisper, for her ears alone, "I am not someone you want to mess with. Trust me. I could punch your lights out, but that's not my style. It's too cliche!

"This city is full of bullies, you know. You need to go find yourself a new act, Brenda. Something original. And while you're at it, try to pick up a personality along the way."

I eyeballed her for another second or two, then backed off and left her standing there, mouth wide-open, cheeks red as ripe tomatoes.

I headed for the girls' room, fear oozing from my pores like sweat, since I was fairly certain Brenda could beat me silly if she had a mind to. And what if she'd surprised me with the jagged edge of a blade? For all I knew she could've been carrying one. I've seen kids around here who do.

CeCe's talent for bluffing has definitely rubbed off on me.

The main thing is, I wanted Brenda to know that I'm easygoing, not gutless, and she understands that now.

I was still boiling mad, though. When I got to the girls' room, I locked myself into an empty stall, and sat there awhile to cool off in privacy.

I wrestled my loose-leaf from my book bag and ripped out a blank sheet. My notebook was in the bag somewhere, but I found the loose-leaf first. I jerked a pen from the bag's side pocket and wrote, in huge letters:

BRENDA MAKES ME SICK.
WHAT IS THIS CHICK'S PROBLEM?
SHE MAKES ME SO ANGRY!

How angry? I asked myself. The writing on the bathroom door gave me a couple of ideas, but using profanity seems lazy to me, as if you can't come up with something better. I closed my eyes and thought of other ways to describe what I was feeling:

I'M SO ANGRY, YOU COULD FRY AN EGG
ON MY HEAD.

Oh, that's *original*, I thought.

I'M SO ANGRY, YOU COULD
BROIL FISH ON MY HEAD,
OR STEAM CLAMS.

76

I hate clams, I thought. *This is silly.* I flung my pen down on the tile floor and screamed. That felt good. Then I retrieved my pen, and sat back down on the toilet.

Why does she have to pick on me? I thought. *Pick, pick, pick. Like a stubborn little bird, pecking away at a tree, in the same, stupid spot, over and over again, as if it's desperate for attention. Or maybe it's determined to leave its mark, no matter how tiny.* Then it came to me:

Brenda is a pesky bird
her sharp beak
peck, peck, pecks away at me
but I'm a tree
a tall and sturdy thing
that she can mark
but never topple

When I started writing, my head felt tight as a brown balloon, but once I finished, I sighed and heard the hiss of hot air escaping. The worst of my anger was gone. I stuck the poem in my loose-leaf book, and went to my English class.

At dinner I told CeCe what had happened with

Brenda, and it got her thinking that maybe the next time she gets mad, she ought to give poetry a try.

"Fine," I said. "But make sure you give me credit for the idea."

LAUGHING IN THE DARK

Some days
are dim
as alleyways
where the streetlights' glow
can't reach
and laughter
is the one and only spark
luminous enough
to pierce
the dark

NOVEMBER 21

I was starved when I got home from school today. Unfortunately all that's left in the cupboard is oatmeal, which I hate, and when I saw that lonely box, unwanted and unopened on the shelf, I threw my hands up, and laughed. My friend Sophie, who was doing homework with me in the kitchen at the time, thought my reaction was a tad strange, but in this house it's considered normal. Besides, the cupboards won't be empty for long. CeCe's out shopping for food right now. Thanksgiving is around the corner, and she plans on fixing a feast. She'll put in a few hours in the kitchen at The Garden this week to make sure she can pay for it. CeCe says it's good to splurge every now and then, since most of the time we're just making do.

Once, when the welfare check I'm embarrassed to admit we need was stolen from our mailbox, CeCe laughed until water filled her eyes, and so did I. When the radiator pipes froze last winter, and we got a cutoff notice from the gas company, we doubled over. Crying was an option, but our tears would have turned into icicles the minute they slid off our lashes, so why bother?

Scarlett O'Hara had the right idea. When Tara burned to the ground, she said, "I'll think about it tomorrow." But before she dropped that famous line, she laughed her head off. At least that's the way I remember it.

Mom doesn't laugh often enough. She's too addicted to drama. She takes everything too seriously. Important things—her job, the men who loved her less than she needed, the failures she can't admit to herself—those I can understand, I guess. But she worries over silly things too. I mean, since when is burnt toast a tragedy? And why sweat it when you accidently over-salt a recipe? Who cares? She does. Too much. Me? I'd laugh, toss the mess in the toilet, wash my hands, and head back to the kitchen for a second try.

Mom used to laugh. A long, long time ago. But somewhere down the road she forgot how. And look where that's gotten her: in a hospital, broken in places nobody but God can fix. I've got no plans on ending up there myself, so I keep laughter and food in the same category, and make sure I get at least three square meals a day.

There are days when laughter hides in the shadows, days when food is low, or Ma Bell disconnects the telephone, or we have no heat and have to layer ourselves in extra socks and sweaters, and sleep cocooned together in every blanket we own. Those are the times when my sense of humor needs a nudge. That's when I fall back on Cosby.

When I was little, I hated thunderstorms. Usually I'd climb in bed with Mom and Dad for comfort, unless they'd had a fight. That was before the divorce, of course, otherwise known as "B.D." If it stormed on a night when they were on the outs, I'd slip into bed with CeCe to keep from being alone. CeCe wasn't wild about having a toddler in her bed, but she felt sorry for me because, with each thunderclap, I'd shiver like a wet puppy. To get my mind off the storm, she'd do whatever it took to get me to giggle—and she still does.

CeCe has a collection of Bill Cosby albums. There's a semi-scary story about a monster called Chicken Heart, and one about Noah that I really like. At one point Noah's talking to God, and trying to weasel out of building the ark, and God says, "N-o-a-h," the way parents say your name when you've done something wrong. You know you're in deep, because they enunciate every single, solitary letter. So Noah says hesitantly, "Yes, Lord?" And after a long pause God asks, "How long can you tread water?" That cracks me up whenever I hear it. But my favorite Bill Cosby story is about him and his brother sharing a bed one night, and how each stakes out his territory. It's CeCe's favorite too. Why else would she use it whenever I need a laugh?

Even now during storms, CeCe's voice will suddenly rise out of the darkness, saying, "This is my side of the bed. Don't be touching my side of the bed." And I smile and answer, "Don't you be touching *my* side!" And we launch into our version of the Cosby skit we've listened to a hundred times sitting in our living room.

The thunder may continue to rattle the windows, and the lightning may dance across the sky a while longer, but laughter robs them of their power to make me afraid.

Man! If there was one thing I could give my mother I'd help her find her smile again. I'd give her laughter.

IT'S JUST A QUESTION

Why study
imaginary numbers
if they don't exist?
I raised my hand
to ask Mr. Peters
this question in class
but he couldn't see past
his pet students
in the front row.
As always,
he pretended
their chairs
were a wall
cutting off
the rest of us.
So I stood
and called
my question out
refusing to let him
make me feel
invisible.

The phrase "It's better to give than to receive" usually sticks in my throat. I've been on the receiving end too few times for the novelty to wear off, I suppose. The Christmas season brings that to mind. CeCe thinks my Christmas spirit is rather stunted, whereas I think hers is overgrown.

There ought to be a law against CeCe haunting used-goods stores this time of year. She sifts through baskets of old-fashioned, hand-stitched decorations as if she's panning for gold, then raids Woolworth's sales bin. Her warped sense of humor drives her to buy outrageously tacky things such as those fat coils of blindingly green tinsel she insists on draping across our windows—the ones facing the street unfortunately. I don't know why I argue for stenciled snowflakes. I never win.

Yesterday Lady Christmas brought home the biggest tree to be found outside of Rockefeller Center. It's slightly smaller than the one she bought last year. The poor living room furniture is huddled in one corner, barely beyond the reach of the tree's sticky branches.

Our apartment is now perfumed in pine, a smell I can't get enough of. The colored lights are doing their dance around the tree, winking off and on, off and on, entertaining me while I'm setting the table for dinner, and I'm thinking, *Yeah, Christmas is okay.* I didn't used to feel that way.

There's not much underneath the tree this year, but CeCe helped me get my best friend, Destinee, something special. My sister's so relieved I'm not hanging out with drug fiends or gang members, she probably chipped in on this gift as a way to reward Destinee for being my friend. I'm just guessing. CeCe might change her mind, though, if she knew about the day Destinee and I spent smoking pot at Carlton's, but she won't hear it from me.

Destinee came over last night to share Christmas Eve dinner with us. The evening would've been perfect except that CeCe got on me about refusing to go with her to see Mom that morning. Come to think of it, that must be my guilt speaking, because all she actually did was mention that Mom had asked for me. In any case, Destinee took my mind off the subject when she looked under the tree. Her eyes popped when she found the gigantic box we'd placed there with her name on it. Of course, before we let her open it, we made her suffer through dinner.

Well, suffer isn't the right word. As always, CeCe had prepared enough food for an army. Turkey, ham stuck with cloves and braised with pineapple juice, corn pudding with a crusty brown glaze, string beans, macaroni and cheese, sweet potato pie. According to my nose, it was Thanksgiving all over again. My mouth wanted to test the theory, but CeCe grabbed her camera and made me wait until she could snap a few pictures of the spread, before the hoards, meaning Destinee and I, descended on the table and picked it clean. She took four or five shots of us at the table as well, then sat down, scooched her chair next to mine for a quick portrait, and turned the camera over to Destinee.

"Smile!" said Destinee, clicking away.

"Okay, okay!" I said. "I'm dying! Let's eat!"

Afterward we cleared the dishes and put the card table away so we'd have room to maneuver. With the Christmas tree hogging so much space, moving around our living room was tricky. CeCe poured each of us a glass of eggnog, then nodded to me. "Now," she said.

I gave Destinee the box with her name on it, and smiled. She set the package on her lap and pierced the tape with her fingernail, careful not to tear the wrapping paper more than necessary. *That's right*, I thought. *Take your time. Be your usual meticulous self.*

Destinee brushed back her blunt-cut bangs, ran a hand through her straight, black Dutch Boy hair, then waded elbow-deep through wads of tissue paper and newspaper strips until she came to a second package. She looked up at me, grinning, and slowly unwrapped the box, stopping to neatly fold the red-and-green foil. Then she gingerly dug through shredded paper, and balls of cotton, and handfuls of confetti until she came to a third, smaller box. This time she raised an eyebrow. I bit my tongue and watched Destinee make her way through boxes four and five. I fought so hard to keep from laughing, I thought lockjaw was imminent. So I opened my mouth and sang, "Chestnuts roasting on an open fire," along with Nat "King" Cole, whose whispery voice floated up from the stereo. "Jack Frost nipping at your nose," I sang at the top of my lungs. I'm a pretty good singer, and I made sure my voice blended with Nat's.

CeCe busied herself cracking walnuts and flicking the shells into a red-and-green dish next to the bowl of nuts on the coffee table. Meanwhile we both kept anxious eyes on Destinee as she shook out each piece of paper, worried that she'd dropped whatever it was we swore we'd gotten for her.

By this point I was ready to concede that maybe I did have a slight mean streak in me, but when Destinee got down on hands and knees to feel underneath the furniture for the gift she was afraid she'd lost, CeCe and I burst out laughing and gave up the game.

While I felt under the tree for Destinee's real gift, CeCe put our "Messiah" album on the turntable. It was Dad's favorite Christmas music, and always makes us think of him. CeCe set the record needle down gently, the album being pretty old and fragile, then she nodded to me.

"Okay," I said to Destinee, giving her a wink. "Open your hands." When she did, I placed a tiny gift in them. It was wrapped in gold foil, in a box the size of a doll's purse. I held my breath while she opened it. Inside was a pearl, set in gold filigree, dangling from a 14-karat chain. I'd picked it out myself. I've been wanting one for the longest time.

Surprise suits some people more than others, and it sure looked good on Destinee last night. When she saw that pearl, her eyes lit like two suns rising, and that light spread across her face until the only thing in the room brighter than the tree was her smile.

It's weird, but the second I saw Destinee's joy, something inside made me wish I had more to give. And not once did it cross my mind to ask, or even care, whether she had any gift for me.

CeCe says there may be hope for me yet.

*A*ll things are possible," CeCe is fond of saying. But she was shocked when I volunteered to visit Mom today. It's December 31st, my last chance to see her before this year is gone completely. "All things in good season," I said. Throwing her words back at her gives me a kick. I don't get to do it often.

I understand why she was so surprised, though. I've put off going to see Mom for a long time, and CeCe knows why.

I hate hospitals.

CeCe and I are experts on the subject of medical institutions. We've visited them often enough. I had to force myself to go when Daddy had his car accident, and he's one person I'd go to the moon for.

Daddy's condition was serious, I knew, because he was in the intensive care unit. His room was easy to find, but hard to enter. I lingered, trembling in the hospital corridor, inches from Daddy's door, light-years away from any sort of peace. "Your daddy's been badly hurt," Mom warned. I asked her if he'd make it. "Honey," she said, "time will tell."

The smell escaping from his room seemed lethal, a

mix of rubbing alcohol and antiseptic designed to fight off disease, though Death himself might squeeze past the sentries at any time.

In three weeks I was an old hand at nonchalantly pushing past the tubes that snaked their way to and from Dad's broken body. (People said his car resembled an accordion.) Whenever I planted a kiss on his forehead, its coolness made me shiver. I couldn't stand to see him that way. Sometimes I'd whisper, *Daddy, please don't leave me.* But the doctors said the brain damage was so extensive that if he lived he would never be the same, and I know he would've hated that, so CeCe and I prayed for him to die, which my aunt thought was a blasphemy. But we loved him best, and death was the kindest thing we could wish for him.

The cruel rhythm of the oxygen machine gave me second thoughts every time its irritating buzz was interrupted by stretches of uneasy silence. My heart pounded out a mini-marathon inside my chest while I held, and held, and held my breath, my teeth clenched of their own volition, until at last that annoying apparatus started up again, wickedly taunting or blessedly assuring me that Daddy would live to see another day.

And then there was Mom, amazing me with her tears. After years of divorce, and two other husbands, there she was crying, and telling Dad that she'd love him forever. "Wouldn't it be great," she said one day, "if you and I could get back together again? You pull through this, I swear, I'll be there for you." Her words must've cut through the semi-coma Dad was in, because he cried.

I looked up at Mom then, and saw love shining in her eyes. They were full of sorrow, but also full of light. Dad died three days later, and so did the light in Mom's eyes. It's the idea of losing the light in mine that worries me the most. I don't want to end up in a mental institution like Mom. The thought of stepping into one gives me the creeps.

I actually know what a vacant stare is, and I wish to God I didn't. But so many of the people in those places have them. They shuffle through the corridors pale as ghosts, and when I walk among them, I imagine I'm the only flesh and blood thing around for miles. The fact that one of those ghosts is my mom makes matters even worse. She *is* my mom, though, and I figured it was time for me to visit.

CeCe went with me, of course. There wouldn't be much point in me going alone, since Mom and I rarely move beyond discussions of the day's barometric pressure. I gave up attempts at meaningful dialogue with her long ago. I need to talk about what's on my mind, and how I feel inside, but Mom has no patience with that sort of thing, and expressions of emotions—hers or anyone else's—practically gives her hives.

The state mental institution Mom is in resembles a penitentiary, which seems about right. Her mental illness is a kind of prison, her mind a place where she keeps hurtful thoughts and feelings locked away. When we entered her room, she was slouched in a corner near the gated window. I almost didn't recognize the girlish stranger, with fresh scrubbed face, and thick cornrows.

"Mom? Look who's here," said CeCe. Mom turned from the window. When her eyes fell on me, they lit up, erasing a bit of the strangeness I felt.

"Hi, baby," she said. Mom, who is not big on touching, reached toward me, her arms trembling and hungry for my hug. I hesitated a second too long for CeCe's taste apparently. She gave me a slight push. *Knock if off,* I said to CeCe with a backward glare. Then I crossed the room, pecked Mom on the cheek, and gave her a squeeze. Her small frame slid into the circle of my arms, and she felt so sheer, it made me gasp. I forget that, of the two of us, I'm the one who's bigger and stronger. It doesn't seem right somehow, and I hate it.

I let my arms drop, afraid to hold her any longer. CeCe suggested we head for the visitors' lounge.

Mom, in a faded blue housedress and paper-thin slippers, walked between us. We passed several patients on the way, one an old gentleman with matted salt-and-pepper hair.

"Morning, Mr. Lewis," said Mom. Mr. Lewis nodded to her and CeCe, smiling, then turned his eyes on me.

"You must be Jazmin," he said. "I wondered when you'd come." My mouth dropped open, and by the time I gathered the words to ask him how he knew my name, he was gone. Mom greeted another patient, a plump lady she called Mrs. Ramirez, with flawless skin the color of flan, and eyes like black marbles, rolling over me from head to toe. She swept me up with a broad and familiar grin, as if I were a long-lost cousin.

"Jazmin," she said, "it's good you come to see your *madre.*"

As soon as Mrs. Ramirez was out of earshot, I tugged Mom's arm. "Okay," I said. "How do these people know who I am?"

"They're in Group with me," she said. "I showed them pictures of you. CeCe brought them on her first visit."

"Group? What's Group?"

"Therapy. We have it once a week."

I was flabbergasted. In all the years of hospital stays, Mom has never agreed to participate in group therapy, even when her doctors at Bellevue begged her to. "I don't believe in all that bleeding in public," she'd say. "Telling strangers your personal business. No. I'd rather keep to myself." Now suddenly Mom's attending Group.

The visiting area was at the far end of the corridor. It consisted of overstuffed love seats and matching chairs, loosely grouped in squares scattered around the room. It was supposed to be cozy, but it felt forced. When you sat there, you had to face the people you were with, which, I suppose, was the point.

I sat on one sofa, glued to CeCe. Mom sat down on the sofa across from us. She waited for me to speak, but my lips weren't moving. My fingers, however, were busy drumming against my knees.

"So, Jazmin, how are you?" she asked. "How have you been?"

"Fine," I said.

"That's good." Silence. "And school? How's school?"

"Pretty good," I said, shrugging. "School is fine."

CeCe, an expert at balancing lopsided conversation, filled the silence with chatter. Mom looked as relieved as I felt.

This is dumb, I thought. *You've come all this way. Say something.*

"What do you do in Group?" I asked abruptly.

"We talk," she said. "About ourselves, our families, the problems that brought us here. And it feels . . . good."

I looked deep into Mom's eyes and found the truth of it, and saw more peace there than I had since Daddy died.

For a long time after the funeral Mom seemed okay. We'd moved to a new apartment in the Bronx, and I was so busy getting settled in my new school, and fighting off my own sorrow, I didn't notice anything wrong with Mom. I mean, I didn't expect any major grieving on her part. Not with all the years they'd been separated. But then one day I came in from the Laundromat, and I was putting clean clothes in her dresser drawer, and found something I wish I hadn't. A pint of gin, tucked between her lingerie. She'd started drinking again, which spelled trouble.

This time I decided to skip the remaining stages of her self-destruct sequence. I telephoned CeCe and asked her to come for me. I've been with her ever since. There was never any question of my staying with Grandma. She's told us often enough that she's got her own life, and there's no room in it for kids.

Mom let me go to CeCe's without much argument. I guess she didn't have any fight left in her. She managed to stay on her feet for a couple more months. Then Grandma got a call from the police one day. They'd found

Mom wandering the streets, snarling at imaginary enemies. Thank God she had her purse and phone book on her, so they knew who to call.

Grandma cried when she signed the commitment papers. Unfortunately the doctors let Mom out two weeks later, once she convinced them she was lucid. But she was back again in a month.

It seems she's been in long enough to make real progress. I mean, my mom in group therapy, bleeding in front of strangers. Man! She may not be talking to me, but at least she's talking to someone. I guess she had to make up her own mind that it was time to get help. No one else could do it for her. Not even me.

Maybe this time she'll get well and stay that way. Maybe.

I reached over and squeezed Mom's hand. She smiled and squeezed mine back. We spoke with our eyes, and let CeCe rattle on for a while without interruption. When it was time to go, CeCe gave her a stack of magazines and paperbacks to read, and I gave her a blank book to write in. I also gave her a hug, this time without any coaxing.

"I'm glad you're getting better, Mom," I whispered. "I love you." Then Mom did the strangest thing. She stepped back, took my face in her hands, and let me see her tears. And she stared deep into me. Not just into my eyes, but deeper, as if she were taking an X ray of my heart.

"I love you too, Jazmin," she said.

Something lodged in my throat and made it difficult for me to swallow. CeCe said good-bye for both of us. She squeezed my shoulder, massaging strength into me, as we walked through the hospital corridor.

I dabbed at my cheeks and looked around for a stair-well.

MOVING DAY

CeCe calls me
her stubborn
flower
bent on
blooming
where I'm
planted.

*C*eCe says the Devil's got no use for people like us because we refuse to stay down for long. We're like those Timex watches. We take a licking and keep on ticking. Our family must be wired that way. Even Mom is starting to show some fight.

During the months since I started this notebook, there've been moments that bore into me like construction workers jackhammering a city street. But like the ground underneath, I'm still here, although my "here" is about to change: CeCe reserved a moving van yesterday.

Come tomorrow we'll be toughing things out further up-town.

I groaned when she announced we'd be relocating, though I wasn't surprised. Two years in the same place? Please! I probably would've tired of this neighborhood soon anyway. I only wish CeCe'd talked with me first. I would've okay'd the move, but I might've suggested waiting until spring. The end of January is too cold for heavy labor, if you ask me. Well, CeCe didn't. But then, I've got so many choices and decisions to make each day, I hardly have time to blink. Maybe it's best CeCe decided this one thing on her own. Whether we move in winter or spring doesn't much matter. There is no good or easy season for saying good-bye.

Usually when it's time to move, I pretend I'm going on vacation, and tell friends I'll see them later. They generally help load the van, so they know the truth. And yet they play the game because they love me and understand how badly I need the fairy tale. Tomorrow it'll be Destinee and Sophie helping me haul boxes to the van.

But—miraculously there is a *but*—I really will be seeing my friends again. In fact, we'll be sharing lunch breaks and assemblies until we graduate, because I informed CeCe that she can ship our belongings to Timbuktu, but I refuse to change schools. Starting over in a new neighborhood, I told her, is tough enough without adding to my adolescent stress.

"Okay, smarty," she said. "Let's move to Zanzibar. Then you can commute by plane."

"Very funny," I said, not laughing. I love my sister, but she's severely warped around the edges. This appears to be another family trait. Luckily, she did agree with me about school.

I'm actually looking forward to our new digs. I'll have a whole room to myself, instead of half of one. And with a door! This is progress, though I suspect nosy CeCe will come and go as she pleases, periodically checking my dresser drawers for drugs to be on the safe side. I hate the invasion of privacy, but she says she's just looking out for me, and I believe her.

Evening is finally settling over Amsterdam Avenue. The blues notes escaping The Garden of Eden have risen several decibels in the last half-hour. Crew is giving the jukebox serious competition, though. He can't sing a lick, but his sad-sounding baritone can be heard a block away. He ought to let B. B. King do all the singing, but no one dares say that to Crew's face. I can't help wondering if it's just me who's seen him gentle, if I'm the only one who knows Crew well enough not to be afraid.

Aunt Sarah stopped to give me a hug on her way upstairs. Her hold was tighter than usual, and I felt warm in the circle of her arms. My hands were freezing, though. Still, I remained on the stoop for as long as I could stand the cold. Sitting on the steps there, keeping tabs on the Avenue one last time, was my own way of saying good-bye.

Well, I better get busy now. I have to clear out my closet, and I've got a few more books to pack, including this one. *The Life and Times of Jazmin Shelby* will still be recorded, but my next entry will have to be in a new notebook because this only has one page left, and I've decided to leave it blank.

There's something about a blank page that makes me tingle. I love how smooth, and crisp, and clean it is. I love how this plain and perfect piece of paper seems to be just waiting for me to baptize it with ink, to put my own special mark on it, to make it mine. And now that I think of it, that's exactly what I love about tomorrows.

Nikki Grimes has applied her prodigious talents to journalism, poetry, novels, photography, and teaching. Her celebrated body of work includes the coming-of-age novel *Growin'*, a Bank Street Children's Book of the Year, and the picture book *It's Raining Laughter*, illustrated with photographs by Myles C. Pinkney. Ms. Grimes won a 1999 Coretta Scott King Honor for *Jazmin's Notebook*. She lives in California.

ML   4/2015